ZEKE'S MARKET

Zucchini

To my sweetheart, Robin Spowart–J.M.
For my father–L.S.J.

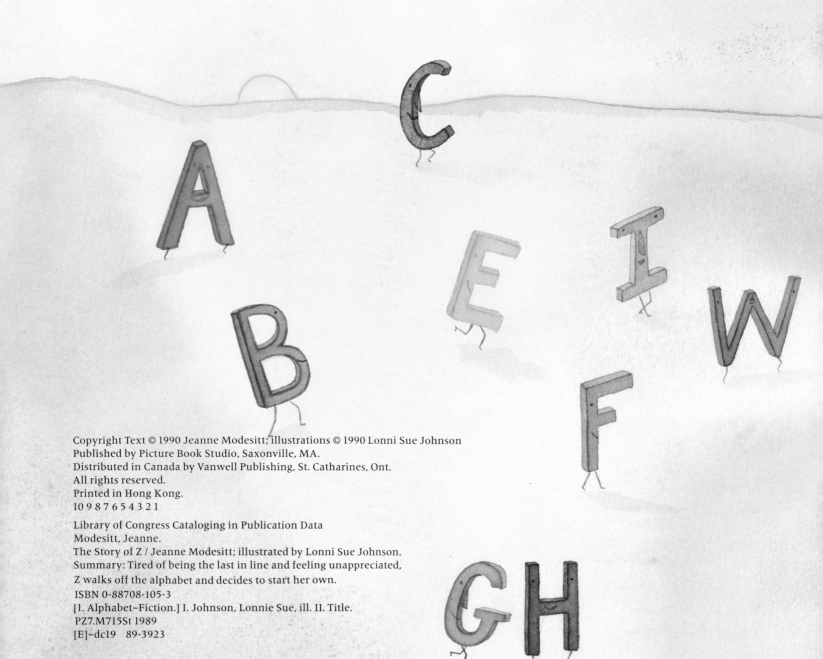

Library of Congress Cataloging in Publication Data
Modesitt, Jeanne.
The Story of Z / Jeanne Modesitt; illustrated by Lonni Sue Johnson.
Summary: Tired of being the last in line and feeling unappreciated,
Z walks off the alphabet and decides to start her own.
ISBN 0-88708-105-3
[1. Alphabet–Fiction.] I. Johnson, Lonnie Sue, ill. II. Title.
PZ7.M715St 1989
[E]–dc19   89-3923

JOSHUA

THE STORY OF Z

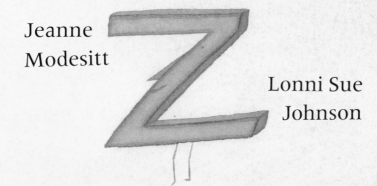

Jeanne
Modesitt

Lonni Sue
Johnson

Picture Book Studio

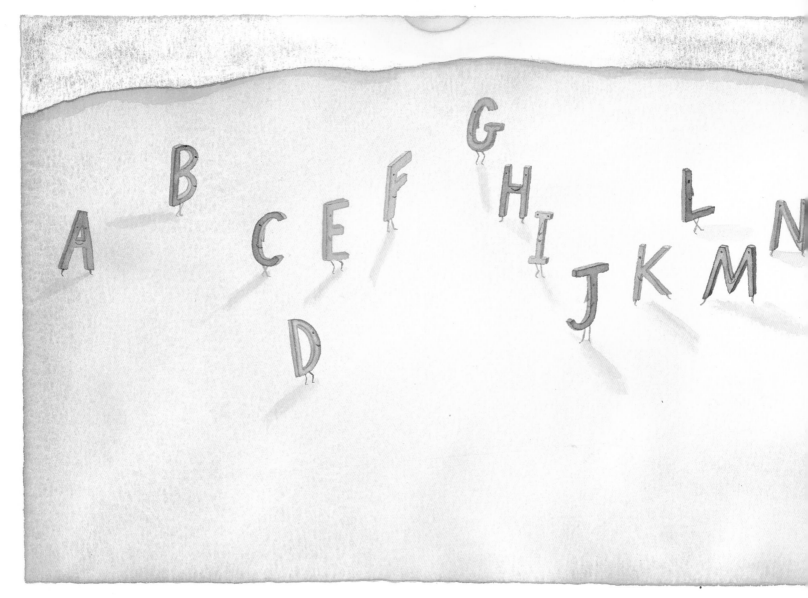

One day, the letter Z walked off the alphabet.

"I'm tired of being last in line," she had complained to X and Y a few minutes earlier. "And my talents just seem to go unnoticed. Why, I'll bet you I'm the least used letter of the entire alphabet. It's enough to make a letter want to leave."

"Z!" gasped X. "How can you say such a thing? You can't leave the alphabet. To do so would be—"

"Mutiny!" cried Y. "Plain and simple mutiny!"

Z tossed her head at Y. "You're just upset because if I were gone, you'd be last in line."

She turned to X. "I've made up my mind. I'm going. Who knows? Maybe I'll start my own alphabet. Coming X?"

X dropped his eyes and said nothing.

"Very well," said Z. "I'm on my own." She sniffed loudly. "But I guess there's nothing new about **that,** is there?"

And off she went.

And the world was not the same without her.

For girls no longer understood boys when they pointed to the sky and said, "Did you see that plane ig-ag as it oomed by?"

Parents frowned at children when they begged, "Can we go to the oo and see the ebras?"

And grandchildren laughed at grandparents when they reminded, "Don't forget to ip up your ippers."

Needless to say, the moment Z left, almost everyone was crying out for her return. Even Y, the most conceited letter of the alphabet, admitted that things had run more smoothly before Z left.

And what did Z think of all this commotion? Well, she was too busy trying to start her own alphabet to even notice it.

But she wasn't having much luck. She couldn't convince any of the letters from the world's different alphabets to join her.

So she began to recruit other types of letters—letters that had never belonged to an alphabet. Unfortunately, such letters rarely do anything for anybody unless there's something in it for them. In fact, the particular letters Z came across were only interested in her idea of starting a new alphabet because they thought the scheme might make them a fast buck, and an easy one at that.

Of course, they didn't tell Z their hidden motives; they simply smiled and nodded and said, "Oh yes, yes, quite a noble plan."

Finally, after Z had made contact with fifteen of these so-called letters, she gathered them together and gave a quick pep talk on how they were about to become the greatest alphabet of all time—with her leading the way, of course.

But the minute she finished her speech and asked, "Now, who would like to be second?"—the letters began to push and shove and the whole thing turned into a brawl.

Z tried to stop the fight but was thrown up into the air, and landed nearby in a pile of leaves.

Moments later, the letters grew tired of fighting and took off in separate directions. Z was still sitting in the pile of leaves, wondering what to do next, when a street sweeper came along.

"Gad ooks!" he said, as he spotted half of Z sticking out from under the pile of leaves. "What have we here?"

Z looked at the sweeper with a frown. "Gad ooks," she repeated irritably. "What kind of word is that?"

"I'm sorry," said the man. "Let me try again. Gad ooks." Then the man began to cry. "You must forgive me," he said. "Life just hasn't been the same since Z left." The man kept on crying and took out a handkerchief.

"People say she was upset because she was last in line and wasn't used as often as the other letters." The man blew his nose. "I guess she didn't understand how important she was."

Z's attention perked. "Just as important as T?" she asked.

"Most certainly."

"As important as A or B or that silly Y?"

"Indeed yes."

Z stood up, throwing off her leaves.

"Z!" the man cried. He ran up and hugged her. "You're back. We've missed you so much. Please, please, won't you come home?"

Z thought for a moment and then dusted herself off. "Very well," she said. "I suppose I'd better. Can't have people running around saying gad ooks to one another."

And off she went…

to rejoin her alphabet.

And that night, for the first time in several weeks,

people could finally go to bed in peace.